CW01511454

ROYAL REEDS

The Playboy

BWWM Erotic Romance

Copyright © 2025 by Royal Reeds

All rights reserved. No part of this publication may be reproduced, stored or transmitted in any form or by any means, electronic, mechanical, photocopying, recording, scanning, or otherwise without written permission from the publisher. It is illegal to copy this book, post it to a website, or distribute it by any other means without permission.

This novel is entirely a work of fiction. The names, characters and incidents portrayed in it are the work of the author's imagination. Any resemblance to actual persons, living or dead, events or localities is entirely coincidental.

First edition

This book was professionally typeset on Reedsy.
Find out more at reedsy.com

Contents

Foreword

So, this was supposed to be a short, super spicy story. Like, eight chapters max. Just straight-up tension, smut, and bad decisions. That's it.

But then...*plot*. Feelings. Character development. WHO ASKED FOR THAT?! NOT I!

Look, leave me alone. I was horny and I have a great imagination. Things got out of hand quickly. And now you're holding a book that's way longer than I intended.

But hey, you're here now. Might as well enjoy the ride.

Happy reading!

Chapter 1

The rhythmic thudding of the headboard against the wall kept time with the pulsating beat of the party outside. Amidst tangled sheets and the scent of lust, Chris drove into her with a ferocity that mirrored his performance on the field. Her breath hitched, a crescendo of pleasure erupting from her lips as her body clenched around him. His green eyes, alight with the thrill of conquest, locked onto hers as he felt the wave overtake him, his muscles tensing in that final moment of release.

"Chris," she moaned, her voice laced with the remnants of ecstasy as he withdrew, leaving her listless. The complaint was sweet music to his ears – another score for the night.

He sauntered into the bathroom, the flush of victory still warm on his skin. Disposing of the condom, he watched it swirl away with an indifference that matched his feelings about the brief encounter. Back in the bedroom, he slid into his pants with practiced ease, the sounds of the party calling him back.

"Will you call me?" she asked, a hopeful note in her voice as she propped herself up on one elbow, her hair a wild halo around her flushed face.

"Maybe," Chris replied with a wink, his trademark grin firmly in place. It was a non-committal promise, a tease wrapped in ambiguity, and before she could press further, he was out the door, swallowed by the sea of bodies gyrating to bass-heavy music.

The next day's classroom was a stark contrast to the sensual atmosphere of the previous evening. Chris sat, half-listening to the drone of the professor's voice, his mind replaying the highlights of his latest triumphs. A subtle vibration from his phone drew his attention; he fished it out discreetly to find a message from his coach blinking on the screen.

"Office. Now." The terse command left no room for argument.

Chris excused himself with a charm-infused apology and made his way to the sanctuary of the football program, the coach's office. Pushing open the door, the smell of leather and musty playbooks greeted him, a familiar pang of adrenaline spiking through his veins.

"Morin," Coach said, not even looking up from the cluttered desk. "Your grades. They're slipping. You want to stay on my team? You pull those numbers up."

Chris leaned against the door frame, his confidence unshaken. "And how do I do that, Coach?"

"Got a tutor lined up for you. Smart kid, top of her class." Coach finally met his gaze, eyes sharp as flint. "She'll whip you into shape, academically speaking. You screw this up, you're benched."

"Understood," Chris replied, the words a smooth veneer over the irritation bubbling beneath the surface. Football was his ticket; no way would he let grades, or anything else jeopardize his future.

Chapter 2

Kira Adams strode into the library, her deep brown eyes scanning the sea of faces for the infamous Christopher Morin. His reputation as the star quarterback was known campus-wide, but his presence in the academic sanctuary was notably absent. Shrugging off the mild irritation that knotted her brow, Kira found a secluded table nestled between the towering bookshelves.

She slid into a chair, her slim, curvy figure folding gracefully under the table, and she meticulously unpacked her backpack. Textbooks lined up like soldiers beside her laptop, her fingers danced across the keyboard with purpose, immersing herself in the world of academia while the clock hands chased each other tirelessly.

An hour trickled by, unaccompanied by an apology or explanation, until the sound of heavy footsteps approached. Kira's focus faltered, her gaze lifting to meet the tardy figure of Chris. He loomed over her with a sheepish grin, extending a hand, "Hey, you must be Kira. I'm Chris."

"An hour late," Kira remarked flatly, not bothering to shake his outstretched hand. She noted how he leaned back slightly, taken aback by her directness.

"Late?" Chris feigned confusion with practiced ease, his charming smile unwavering. "Sorry about that, something came up. You know how it is."

Kira's eyes narrowed, unamused by the act. She could see through his façade, recognizing the all-too-familiar play of the charismatic athlete. But this was no game to her, and she was not one to be played.

Kira snapped her textbook shut, the sound echoing her mounting frustration. "You 'know how it is,' Chris? Because from where I'm sitting, it looks like you don't know—or care—how important this is." Her tone was as sharp as the angle of her jaw, set in defiance. She rose to her feet, nearly matching his height with her indignant posture.

"Let me introduce myself properly," she continued, her deep brown eyes unyielding. "I'm Kira Adams, your tutor. And my time, as well as yours, is valuable. You're not just jeopardizing your own future in football, but also the pay that I was promised for helping you."

She paused, letting her words hang in the air between them, the weight of her expectations clear and non-negotiable. "Next time, be on time, Chris. I'm not here to play games or babysit. Are we clear?" Kira's voice was steady, commanding respect—a reflection of her unshakeable resolve to succeed and demand nothing less from those around her.

Chapter 3

Kira sat across from Chris in the library, her laptop open, highlighting notes in her textbook while he scratched something down in his notebook. She expected the usual—him zoning out, cracking jokes, or finding some excuse to avoid the work.

But when she glanced over, she did a double take.

His notes were...organized. His handwriting, while a little messy, was legible. And, most surprisingly, he was actually focused.

"You've been studying on your own," she blurted, brows lifting in surprise.

Chris looked up, flashing that cocky, dimpled smirk. "What, you think I just roll out of bed and wing it?" He leaned back in his chair, stretching his arms behind his head. "I'm not a superstar athlete for nothing, Adams. I put in the work."

Kira stared at him for a beat, then shook her head with a small, reluctant smile. "Huh. Guess there's more to you than just a pretty face."

"Damn, was that a compliment? Be careful, Adams, I might get used to that."

She rolled her eyes, but he caught the way her lips twitched, like she was fighting back a laugh. He liked that look on her, liked getting that reaction from her.

He tapped his pen against his notebook. "Hey, we should exchange numbers."

That made her raise a skeptical brow. "Why?"

Chris gave her a deadpan look. "In case I have a question. Or need help. You know, normal tutor stuff?"

Kira narrowed her eyes, as if trying to see through him, but he only grinned in response, his green eyes twinkling with mischief. Finally, with a quiet sigh, she pulled out her phone.

"Fine," she said, handing it over.

Chris took it, fingers brushing against hers—just barely, but enough to send a little jolt through her. He smirked like he knew it, too, and quickly typed his number in before passing it back.

"There," he said. "Now, if I ever need saving from a particularly tough assignment, you're just a text away."

Kira huffed a small laugh, shaking her head. "We'll see if you actually use it for studying."

Chris pressed a hand to his chest, mock-offended. "You wound me, Adams. I'm a changed man."

She didn't believe that for a second. But as she glanced down at her phone, at the new contact sitting in her list, Chris Morin, she had to admit…

Maybe she didn't mind too much.

Chapter 4

Two days later, Kira walked up the steps of the campus library, adjusting the strap of her bag. The evening air was crisp, the faint hum of students chatting and footsteps on pavement filling the background. She pulled her phone out and sent a quick text to Chris.

Kira: *I'm here. Where are you?*

She waited, arms crossed against the slight chill, until her phone buzzed.

Chris: *Change of plans, Adams. The library's closed, a power outage. Study session's postponed unless...*

She frowned. *Unless?*

Kira: *Unless what?*

Chris: *Unless you wanna study at my place.*

Kira stared at the message, chewing on her lip. Study at his apartment? That sounded like a bad idea. A very, very bad idea.

Kira: *I don't know, Chris...*

Chris: *What, you don't trust me? I'm an excellent host.*

Kira: *I find that hard to believe.*

Chris: *Come on, Adams. I promise to be on my best behavior.*

She sighed. She really needed to help him pass, and if the library wasn't an option...

Kira: *Fine. One study session at your place. That's it.*

Chris: *Looking forward to it, Teach.*

She rolled her eyes but couldn't help the small smile that played at her lips.

Kira stood outside Chris's apartment door, notebook in one hand, phone in the other, debating whether or not this was a mistake. But before she could knock, the door swung open.

And there he was.

Shirtless.

Chris leaned against the doorframe, his toned, ridiculously sculpted chest on full display. His dark brown hair was damp, like he'd just gotten out of the shower, and his signature smirk was already in place.

Kira immediately turned her head, staring hard at the wall like it was the most fascinating thing she'd ever seen.

"Oh my God, Chris. Seriously?"

He chuckled. "What? It's my apartment."

She exhaled sharply. "Put on a shirt."

"Why?" he teased, crossing his arms over his very distracting abs. "Is it bothering you?"

She turned back to glare at him, a big mistake—because now he was flexing just a little, clearly enjoying himself.

"It's distracting me," she muttered, pushing past him into the apartment.

Chris laughed as he shut the door. "Alright, alright. Give me a sec."

While he disappeared into his bedroom, Kira took in her surroundings. She expected chaos, maybe clothes thrown over furniture, empty pizza boxes, and the general disaster zone that most guys' places tended to be.

But it was shockingly clean.

The sleek black couch was spotless, the coffee table neatly arranged, and a faint scent of fresh laundry lingered in the air.

Chris walked back out, now in a fitted t-shirt, rubbing the back of his neck. "See? Not a slob."

Kira glanced around again and hummed. "I'm honestly impressed."

Chris smirked, sitting down on the couch. "Told you I'm full of surprises."

She rolled her eyes but joined him, opening her notebook. "Let's just get started."

For a while, they actually did study. Chris asked questions, took notes, and didn't once try to flirt. Kira was dare she say it, proud of him.

But then he caught her staring when he absentmindedly stretched, the hem of his shirt riding up just enough to reveal the cut of his abs.

"You sure you don't want me to take the shirt off?" he teased.

Kira groaned, throwing her pencil at him. "Oh my God, Chris!"

He dodged it easily, grinning. "What? You were staring."

"I was not staring."

"You totally were."

She crossed her arms, feigning exasperation. "You're insufferable."

"And yet," he said, leaning closer with a smirk, "you keep hanging out with me."

Kira opened her mouth for a retort but shut it just as quickly. He had a point. Instead, she huffed, looking away. "Just focus."

Chris chuckled but let it go, shifting back into study mode.

After another hour, Kira stretched and got up, wandering around his living room. Her eyes landed on a small shelf lined with trophies. Some dusty, some polished and gleaming. Beside them were framed photos of a much younger Chris, grinning ear to ear, standing next to a man who had the same green eyes.

Chris walked up beside her. "That's my dad."

Kira glanced up at him, surprised by the softness in his voice. "You guys look close."

Chris picked up one of the trophies, running a thumb over the engraved plate. "We were. He was my biggest fan growing up. I still remember my first touchdown when I was eight—he damn near lost his mind. Swore I was gonna be the next NFL legend."

Kira watched him carefully, sensing the weight behind his words. Football wasn't just a sport to him, it was his connection to his father.

She smiled gently. "Sounds like he was really proud of you."

Chris nodded, setting the trophy back down. "Yeah. He was."

For a moment, they stood there, the space between them smaller than it had been all evening.

Kira's breath hitched as she realized just how close they were, how his gaze had shifted from playful to something heavier, more intense.

No. Nope. Not happening.

She cleared her throat, stepping back. "I should, um… I should probably go."

Chris blinked, as if snapping out of something, then nodded slowly. "Right. Yeah."

She grabbed her bag, avoiding his eyes. "Thanks for, uh… actually studying this time."

Chris smirked, back to his usual self. "Anything for my favorite tutor."

Kira rolled her eyes but couldn't fight the warmth creeping up her neck as she headed for the door.

As she left, she swore she heard him chuckle under his breath.

And she hated how much she wanted to hear it again.

Chapter 5

The gym smelled like sweat and iron, the rhythmic clanking of weights filling the air as Chris and his teammates pushed through another grueling workout. The wide mirrors along the walls reflected their intensity, sweat-soaked shirts, flexed muscles, and the occasional grunt of exertion.

But Chris?

Chris was distracted.

Sitting on a weight bench, he wiped the sweat off his face with his shirt before glancing at his phone. A new text lit up the screen.

Kira: *I still don't understand how someone who memorizes plays so easily struggles with basic history facts.*

Chris smirked, already typing a response.

Chris: *Because, Adams, history is about the past. Football is about the future. Obviously.*

A second later, his phone buzzed again.

Kira: *That was the dumbest thing I've ever read.*

Chris: *And yet, you keep texting me. Admit it, you love my genius.*

Chris chuckled, shaking his head.

"Bro… you've been smiling at that phone for a solid five minutes."

Chris glanced up to see his teammate, Jordan, watching him with raised brows, a smirk creeping onto his face.

"Man's got his eye on his next target," another teammate, Malik, teased, nudging Jordan. "Who is she, Morin? Another cheerleader? Someone from your fan club?"

Chris rolled his eyes, setting his phone down on the bench beside him. "Relax, it's just my tutor."

Jordan scoffed. "Since when do you text tutors with that dopey-ass smile?"

Chris shot him a look but said nothing, rubbing his towel over his hair.

Malik leaned against a machine, arms crossed. "Alright, let's hear it. Who is she?"

Chris hesitated for half a second—just enough for Jordan's grin to widen.

"Ohh, this is different," Jordan said, pointing at him. "You actually like this one."

Chris huffed out a laugh. "Shut up."

Jordan and Malik exchanged a knowing look before Malik said, "You might be able to fool the girls, man, but we've known you too long. You don't text like this unless you're interested."

Chris grabbed his phone, already feeling his teammate's teasing closing in. He opened Kira's message, ignoring the fact that his stupid grin was back.

Chris: *You're just mad because I'm hilarious.*

Kira: *Hilariously annoying.*

Chris bit his lip, shaking his head as he typed.

Chris: *Annoyingly charming.*

Kira didn't respond right away, and for some reason, he waited, his fingers tapping against his thigh.

When his phone finally buzzed, he unlocked it immediately.

Kira: *Keep telling yourself that, Morin.*

He exhaled a quiet laugh.

Jordan and Malik groaned. "Man, you're down bad."

Chris just smirked. "Shut up and lift, losers."

But as he went back to his workout, he couldn't fight the grin that stayed glued to his face.

Chapter 6

The pulsing bass of the club reverberated through Chris's muscular frame as he shouldered his way through the throng of bodies. Connor's birthday bash was in full swing, the air thick with the scent of sweat and expensive cologne. With a practiced smile and a nod here and there to acquaintances, he made his way to the VIP area where his teammates lounged like kings surveying their court.

"Morin!" Connor bellowed over the music, raising a glass in salute. "You made it!"

"Wouldn't miss it for the world," Chris shouted back, clapping a hand on Connor's shoulder before scanning the room with those piercing green eyes that missed nothing.

That's when he saw her—a woman standing at the fringe of their group, her laughter ringing clear even amidst the music. She had a way about her, a magnetic pull he felt in his bones. Chris approached her with the confidence of a man who knew his worth, his dark hair tousled just so.

"Hey," he said, voice smooth despite the surrounding noise. "I'm Chris."

Her response was lost in the beat of the music, but her smile spoke volumes. They talked, or rather, shouted pleasantries and flirtatious quips. Each time she laughed, it was like a siren call, and Chris found himself wanting to hear it in a setting that wasn't drowned out by DJ mixes and partygoers.

"Want to get out of here?" he asked, leaning in close.

She nodded, eyes alight with anticipation.

The cool night air hit them as they left the club, the muffled thumps of music fading behind them. They walked together, an electric current running between them, until they reached his apartment.

No sooner had Chris closed the door behind them that they came together, lips crashing with a hunger that had been building since their first eye contact. With each step toward the bedroom, clothing fell away like discarded shields, revealing taut skin and the promise of what was to come.

They collapsed onto the bed in a tangle of limbs, his broad shoulders casting shadows across her body in the dim light. Her giggles filled the room, a melody more intoxicating than any club track, as they surrendered to the moment, to the reckless abandon that defined so many of Chris's nights.

Yet tonight, there was something different in the air, something that whispered of potential changes on the horizon. For now, however, all that mattered was the connection of two bodies moving in unison, chasing a pleasure that only the night could offer.

Bathed in the glow of neon lights filtering through the bedroom window, Chris's gaze followed the arch of her back as she shifted beneath him. The anticipation palpable, he watched with a wolfish grin as she welcomed him with an inviting spread of her thighs, unveiling the delicate pink that beckoned him closer. His groan vibrated through the charged air, low and primal, as he gripped his length, guiding himself to her warmth.

"Jesus," she gasped, her breath catching at the feel of him pressing inside her, stretching her walls. "You're—"

"Too big?" His chuckle rumbled from deep within his chest, an undercurrent of pride threading through the amusement. With a teasing smirk, he leaned down, whispering against her lips, "Don't worry, I'll take good care of you."

And with those words, he set forth a rhythm that was both deliberate and gentle, adjusting to the snug fit. Soon enough, as their bodies demanded more, his pace quickened, their movements becoming a frenzied dance of flesh on flesh. They climbed together, higher and higher, until they crested in a crashing wave of mutual release, leaving them both panting, spent, and entwined.

As their breathing slowed, the room once again filled with the quiet sounds of the city below. Chris rolled off to lie beside her, his mind already drifting as he reached for the phone lying abandoned on the nightstand. He swiped the screen, his green eyes scanning for any sign of a message from Kira. Nothing. A twinge of something unrecognizable flickered in his chest—a mix of anticipation and an odd sense of longing.

The woman began to collect her clothes, slipping into them with a practiced ease that spoke of many such nights. Her voice cut through his thoughts, "I should get going."

"Okay," Chris murmured absently, still transfixed by the silent device in his hand. He didn't watch her dress; instead, his thumb idly scrolled through his feed, feigning indifference. Only when she stood waiting did he rise, crossing the room to escort her out with a nonchalance that failed to reach his eyes.

"Thanks," she said, a hint of satisfaction in her tone as she stepped through the doorway.

"Anytime," he replied smoothly, but his mind was elsewhere. As the door clicked shut behind her, he returned to his bed, reclining against the cool sheets. His body was still warm from their encounter, but his attention remained glued on his phone, on the possibility of a text from Kira that would send his heart into an erratic sprint.

In the silence of his apartment, Chris lay there, a man who could have any woman he desired yet found himself inexplicably ensnared by the one who eluded him. As the night deepened, he waited for a sign, a word, anything from Kira, not realizing that in his pursuit of distraction, it was her absence that haunted him most.

Chapter 7

Chris sat in the lecture hall, gripping his pen as he scanned the last few questions on the test in front of him. His knee bounced slightly under the desk, but for the first time in a long time, it wasn't from nerves.

Because he actually knew the answers.

As he read through the questions, he could hear Kira's voice in his head, patiently explaining the material during their late-night study sessions.

"No, Chris, you can't just guess. Think. Connect it to something that makes sense to you."

He smirked, filling in another answer. He'd give her credit, she was a damn good tutor.

By the time he finished, a rare sense of confidence settled over him. He didn't just wing this test. He actually knew his stuff. And that? That deserved a celebration.

As soon as he turned in his paper, he pulled out his phone and shot off a text.

Chris: *Adams, I'm 90% sure I just passed that test. Let's hit the club tonight to celebrate.*

He slung his bag over his shoulder and walked out of the lecture hall, weaving through students. By the time he reached the main hallway, his phone buzzed.

Kira: *That's not really my thing.*

Chris rolled his eyes, grinning. *Of course she'd say that.*

Chris: *Come on. You've been busting your ass helping me. Let me show you a good time.*

The three little dots appeared. Then disappeared. Then appeared again.

Chris chuckled. *She's thinking about it.*

Finally, after what felt like forever, his phone lit up again.

Kira: *Fine. But if this is a terrible idea, I'm blaming you.*

Chris's grin stretched wide.

Chris: *Don't worry, Adams. You're in good hands.*

He slipped his phone into his pocket, still smirking to himself.

Then he heard her voice.

"Chris!"

He turned to see Molly Hayes his previous girlfriend of a mere three weeks strutting toward him, long blonde waves bouncing, a flirtatious smile already in place. His previous girlfriend of a mere three weeks.

Oh, great.

"Hey, Molly." He kept his tone casual, but she didn't miss a beat, stepping in a little too close.

"So, what are you up to tonight?" she asked, tilting her head, blue eyes scanning his face. "Wanna grab drinks? I was thinking we could—"

"Can't," Chris cut in smoothly. "Made plans."

Molly's lips pursed slightly, her fingers twirling a strand of hair. "Oh?" She leaned in, curious. "With who?"

Chris smirked, watching the way her eyes narrowed slightly, like she was already piecing things together.

"That," he said, tapping a finger against his temple, "is a secret."

Molly's jaw tightened just a little, but she quickly masked it with a practiced smile.

"Hmm," she hummed, stepping back. "Well, have fun."

Chris just shot her a wink before walking away, his phone already in his hand, ready to text Kira again.

Tonight was going to be interesting.

Chapter 8

Kira stood in front of her mirror, smoothing down the fabric of her dress. The square-neck, long-sleeve mini-dress fit her perfectly, hugging her curves in a way that made her feel confident— something she hadn't expected. She'd bought it months ago, thinking she'd eventually have an occasion to wear it.

Tonight, apparently, was that occasion.

She grabbed her black heels, slipping them on, then checked her phone.

Chris: *I'm outside.*

She took a deep breath, grabbed her purse, and hurried out the door.

The moment she stepped outside, Chris Morin was the first thing she saw.

He was leaning against his black car, arms crossed, looking effortlessly sexy in a navy blue button-up and dark jeans. The top few buttons were undone, revealing just a hint of his toned chest, and the sleeves were rolled up to his forearms.

Kira slowed her steps when she noticed something unusual, he was staring.

His usual cocky smirk was gone. Instead, his jaw was slightly slack, his green eyes slowly raking over her from head to toe.

She shifted, suddenly feeling warm under his gaze. "Chris?"

He blinked, snapping out of it. "Shit—uh, yeah." He cleared his throat, rubbing the back of his neck. "You look… amazing."

Kira pressed her lips together, trying to ignore the way her stomach flipped. "Thanks."

Chris opened the passenger door for her. "Come on, Adams. Let's go celebrate my academic genius."

She rolled her eyes but couldn't hide the small smile as she slid into the car.

Inside the club, the bass thrummed through the floor, neon lights casting a soft glow over the packed dance floor. Kira hadn't been to a place like this in a while, and she wasn't sure she'd ever been to one with someone like Chris Morin.

Chris led her through the crowd, his hand resting lightly on her lower back, guiding her toward the bar. He leaned in close so she could hear him over the music.

"What are you drinking?"

She made a face. "I hate the taste of alcohol."

Chris smirked. "Then you're gonna love this one."

He turned to the bartender. "Sour Amaretto for her."

A moment later, the drink was placed in front of her. She hesitated before taking a sip—then her eyes widened. It was sweet, citrusy, and smooth, the kind of drink that went down way too easily.

Chris grinned. "Told you."

"Okay, I'll admit it. This is actually good," she said, taking another sip.

After another drink, Chris took her hand. "Come on, let's dance."

Kira almost protested, but then she saw the challenge in his eyes.

"You sure you can keep up, Morin?" she teased.

His brows lifted. "Guess we'll find out."

She let him lead her to the dance floor, the beat pulsing around them. At first, he was the one guiding her, his hands settling on her waist as they moved to the rhythm. But then Kira started moving, and Chris froze for half a second.

She was good. No, she was damn good.

"You're a dancer?" he asked over the music, watching as she moved effortlessly, her body fluid and completely in sync with the beat.

Kira smirked, twirling once before stepping in closer. "What, you thought I was just a nerd?"

Chris let out a low chuckle. "Gotta admit, Adams, you keep surprising me."

Before he could say more, a familiar voice called out.

"Yo, Morin!"

Chris turned to see David, one of his teammates, making his way toward them, a drink in hand.

David's gaze flicked between them, a slow smirk forming. "Didn't know you had a date tonight."

Kira immediately shook her head. "We're not dating."

Chris, at the same time, said, "No, man, it's not like that."

David raised an eyebrow. "Uh-huh."

Kira crossed her arms. "I'm just his tutor."

David nodded slowly, clearly not believing either of them. "Sure. Strictly academic, I get it." Then he winked and clapped Chris on the shoulder. "Have fun with your *studying*, bro."

As he walked off, two women already draping themselves over him, Kira and Chris turned to each other.

Then burst out laughing.

"Think he bought it?" Chris asked, still grinning.

Kira shook her head, amused. "Not a chance."

Chris smirked. "Guess we're just that convincing."

Kira rolled her eyes, taking another sip of her drink. But even as she laughed, she couldn't ignore the fact that for one brief moment, when David assumed they were together...

Neither of them had rushed to correct him.

Chapter 9

The ride back was quieter, but not in an awkward way. It was the kind of silence that felt comfortable, the kind that came when two people weren't in a rush to fill the space with empty words. The night had been unexpectedly good, and neither of them seemed ready for it to end just yet.

Chris tapped his fingers against the steering wheel, glancing over at Kira as they drove. "Alright, Adams. I feel like I don't know nearly enough about you."

Kira raised a brow. "What do you mean? You know I'm a tutor, I like dancing, and I don't drink."

Chris smirked. "Yeah, but that's surface-level stuff. What's the big picture?"

Kira exhaled, watching the city lights blur past the window. "I want to be a teacher," she said after a moment. "It's all I've ever wanted. I had some really amazing teachers growing up, and they changed my life. I want to do the same for someone else."

Chris nodded, his expression thoughtful. "That's... really cool, actually."

She smiled, nudging him lightly. "Alright, your turn. What's your big goal?"

He let out a soft chuckle. "I mean, kinda obvious, don't you think?"

She rolled her eyes. "Other than making it to the NFL, Chris."

Chris hesitated for a second before shrugging. "I guess… I just want to make my dad proud. He put everything into my career. Football's always been our thing."

Kira studied him, hearing the unspoken weight in his words. "You think he wouldn't be proud of you already?"

Chris swallowed, gripping the steering wheel a little tighter. "I don't know. He had big dreams for me. I just don't wanna let him down."

Kira didn't know what to say to that—so she didn't say anything, just let the conversation settle between them.

Chris suddenly turned the car off the main road, driving up a steep incline.

Kira frowned. "Where are we going?"

"You'll see."

A few minutes later, he pulled into a small clearing at the top of a hill. When Kira looked out her window, her breath caught.

The entire city stretched out before them, lights twinkling against the night sky, the skyline glowing in the distance.

Chris leaned back, watching her reaction. "Figured you'd like it."

Kira turned to him, genuinely impressed. "I didn't peg you for the 'romantic view' type."

He smirked. "I contain multitudes, Kira."

She laughed softly, then turned back to the view, taking in the peacefulness of it all. For a moment, neither of them spoke, just sat there, watching the world below.

Eventually, Chris glanced at her and grinned. "Alright, Cinderella. Let's get you home before you turn back into a pumpkin."

She rolled her eyes but didn't argue.

When they reached her apartment, Chris parked and walked her to the door. The night air was cool, but Kira felt warm, an odd mix of emotions swirling in her chest.

She turned to him. "Thanks for tonight. I actually had... a lot of fun."

Chris tilted his head, smirking. "Was that so hard to admit?"

Kira huffed a laugh. "Yes."

He chuckled, shoving his hands into his pockets. "Guess I'll just have to make sure you have fun more often."

Kira shook her head, smiling. Then, before she could overthink it—before she could talk herself out of it—she stepped closer.

And kissed him.

It wasn't a hesitant kiss. It was soft, slow, sensual—a lingering press of lips that sent a slow, dangerous heat curling in her stomach.

Chris stiffened for a brief second, as if caught off guard, but then he kissed her back, his hands twitching at his sides like he wanted to pull her closer but was waiting for permission.

When she finally pulled away, her heart was racing.

Her eyes widened as reality slammed into her.

"Oh, God." She stepped back, pressing a hand to her forehead. "That was… that was a bad idea."

Chris blinked, still looking stunned. "Kira—"

But before he could say anything, she fumbled for her keys, turned, and hurried inside, shutting the door behind her.

She pressed her back against it, breathing hard, her mind spinning.

What the hell had she just done?

And worse…

Why did she already want to do it again?

Chapter 10

Chris's fingers drummed an anxious rhythm on the wooden table, a stark contrast to his usual composed demeanor. The library was quiet except for the occasional rustle of pages turning and the soft hum of whispers. He glanced at the clock; it was almost time for Kira to walk through those doors. She'd stride in with her dark curls bouncing, her brown eyes laser-focused, ready to dive into textbooks and lecture notes.

He couldn't quite shake the memory of their last meeting—the unexpected kiss that seemed to have altered the gravitational pull between them. The nervous anticipation was new to him, a feeling he wasn't comfortable with.

The doors swung open, and there she was, dressed in her usual casual attire that somehow still managed to highlight the curves he was trying not to think about. Without acknowledging the electric tension hanging in the air, Kira sat down opposite him and started laying out her materials methodically.

"Kira," Chris broke the silence, his voice surprisingly steady despite the adrenaline rush. "About Friday—"

She looked up from her books, her expression unreadable. "It was a mistake," she interrupted curtly, "and it won't happen again. We're here to study, let's keep it that way."

"Sure, sure," Chris replied with a shrug, the corner of his mouth lifting into a half-smirk. "You wouldn't be able to handle me anyway."

Her brows knitted together, a flicker of irritation in her deep brown eyes. "What's that supposed to mean?" she demanded, her voice low but sharp.

Chris leaned back in his chair, a chuckle escaping him. "No offense, but I don't do virgins."

Kira gasped, clearly annoyed. "That's what you think? That I'm a virgin?" she countered, her cheeks flushed with a mix of anger and indignation.

"Oh yeah," he said, teasingly drawing out the words.

"Chris," Kira began, her tone more steely than before, "for your information, I'm not a virgin. I've had at least two boyfriends."

"Having boyfriends doesn't mean you can handle me," he retorted, his smirk growing as he watched her reaction closely.

"Handle what, exactly?" Kira's voice was even, but there was a challenge in her gaze now.

"I fuck, Kira, hard," Chris stated bluntly, his eyes locked onto hers, gauging her response.

There was a momentary catch in her breath, a subtle swallow as she processed his words. Then, with an unwavering stare, she leaned forward slightly and said confidently, "I could handle you."

As their eyes met, a silent recognition passed between them—a spark, an unspoken understanding that they were both playing with fire.

The tension between them was a palpable force, an electric current that buzzed through the air. Chris leaned forward, his arms folded on the table as he regarded Kira with that characteristic smirk, the one that had undone so many before her.

"Let's make a deal," he said, the words rolling off his tongue like a challenge. His green eyes danced with mischief, a silent dare for her to rise to the bait.

Kira's posture stiffened, her studious facade momentarily slipping in the face of his proposition. "What kind of deal?" she asked, though her voice betrayed a hint of curiosity.

"Simple." He unfolded his arms and gestured casually between them. "We fuck. And if you reach the breaking point first, you have to admit you can't handle me."

There it was, the gauntlet thrown down at her feet. The heat in his gaze was intense, expectant, waiting for her response.

For a moment, she seemed to weigh her options, her chest rising and falling with a deep breath. Then, with a defiance that seemed to match his own, she squared her shoulders and met his stare unflinchingly. "Agreed."

With those words hanging between them, the deal was struck, an agreement laced with bravado and an undercurrent of something far more dangerous. Something neither of them fully understood yet.

Chapter 11

Kira's back met the softness of Chris' bed with an unceremonious bounce, her breath hitching as she watched him strip away his shirt with a fluidity that spoke volumes of his confidence. The fabric fell to the floor with a whisper, revealing the sculpted planes and valleys of his muscles. She tried to suppress the desire that licked through her veins like wildfire, but it was no use—her body responded with an intensity that was almost embarrassing.

"Like what you see?" Chris' voice was a low rumble, his smirk predatory as he caught the way she bit her lip, a futile attempt to contain her arousal.

Nodding was beyond her, words lost in the heat swirling inside her. He was on her in an instant, the weight of him both intimidating and exhilarating. His lips found hers, initially gentle, tasting her with a patience she hadn't expected from him. But soon enough, gentleness gave way to hunger, his mouth roaming over her neck, sucking at her skin until she was certain it would leave a mark.

She felt a dampness growing between her thighs again, a testament to the effect he had on her. Chris seemed to sense it too, his hands boldly exploring, kneading her breast over her blouse before nimbly undoing the buttons, peeling the fabric away with an ease that suggested this wasn't his first rodeo. Her chest rose and fell rapidly, encased in a lacy baby blue bra that suddenly felt too constricting under his heated gaze.

"You're beautiful," he breathed against her skin, his fingers tracing the outline of the lace before unclasping her bra with practiced dexterity. Cool air kissed her nipples just a moment before Chris did, his mouth warm and insistent as he sucked each one in turn, drawing moans from her lips that echoed off the walls.

Her body arched into him, seeking more contact, more of the delicious friction he was creating. But he was already moving on, his hands sliding down to her shorts and panties, stripping them away in one swift motion. She heard his groan, rich and primal, as he discovered the glistening evidence of her desire.

Then she saw it—the thick length of his cock as he freed himself from his jeans. Panic fluttered in her chest; it looked massive, far larger than anything she'd encountered before, and instinctively, she scooted back on the bed.

"Hey," Chris said, a firm note in his voice as he grabbed her ankle and reeled her back toward him. "Don't run from me."

The command in his tone sent another shiver through her, one that was equal parts anxiety and anticipation. Chris held her gaze, intense and unwavering, the unspoken promise clear in his eyes: he would take care of her, even if his size intimidated her now. Kira's heart pounded in her chest, caught between the fear of the unknown and the thrill of what was to come.

Trembling with hesitance, Kira's voice was barely a whisper as she voiced her fear. "It's not going to fit."

Chris paused, his eyes locking onto hers with a confidence that bordered on arrogance. A single eyebrow arched in challenge as he reached into the nightstand drawer and retrieved a condom. "Trust me," he countered smoothly, "it will."

Her breath hitched as she watched him roll the latex down over his engorged length, a silent prayer whispered for her own endurance. With a gentle nudge, he parted her trembling legs and guided himself to her entrance. As he pushed inside, the sensation overwhelmed her, stretching her to her limits, and her fingers instinctively dug into his forearms.

"Shit," Chris hissed under his breath, the tightness enveloping him like a vice. "You're so tight."

Kira could only manage a whimper in response, her body taut with the effort of accommodating him. "I'm not tight... you're just too big," she breathed out, her voice laced with a mixture of pain and awe.

He leaned down, his face inches from hers, intensity burning in his green eyes. "I'm not even all the way in yet, Kira." His tone was gruff, but not without tenderness.

A string of curses left her lips before she could stop them, her body rigid with the strain. Sensing her tension, Chris murmured for her to relax, but her muscles remained locked.

Seeing her struggle, Chris shifted tactics. He lowered his head, capturing her lips in a deep kiss, his tongue seeking hers with a passion meant to distract and soothe. Their tongues entwined in an intimate dance, coaxing her to let go of her fears.

As she finally melted into the kiss, he slid deeper, filling her completely. A loud moan vibrated against his mouth, signaling her surrender to the sensation.

"Good girl," he whispered against her lips, beginning to move within her. Her body, now compliant beneath his, responded to each thrust, her initial discomfort transforming into pleasure.

"Doing well so far," he praised softly, his rhythm steady and measured.

With every push and pull, pleasure built within her, erasing the lines of worry from her brow. Her eyes fluttered shut, lashes casting shadows on her flushed cheeks. The room filled with the soundtrack of their union; Chris's controlled grunts mingling with Kira's escalating moans. He increased his pace, watching as she lost herself in the sensation, her jaw slackening as moans slipped unbidden from her lips.

The rhythm of their bodies became a primal drumbeat, an insistent pulse that drove them both toward oblivion. "That feel good?" Chris grunted, his voice rough with desire as he slammed into her with a force that sent ripples through the mattress.

Kira's response was a moan, deep and guttural, spilling from her parted lips. Her head tossed back on the pillow, eyes squeezed shut, she could only nod, words lost in the haze of pleasure that was beginning to cloud her mind.

"Fuck you feel so hot," he growled, his pace relentless, each thrust deeper, more commanding than the last. She felt the heat of him, the power of his muscular form pressing her down into the softness of his bed, enveloping her in sensation.

Chris's hands roamed over her body, stoking the fire within her until it raged out of control. And then, with a few final, punishing strokes, he pushed her over the edge. Kira shuddered violently, her inner walls clenching around him as waves of ecstasy broke over her.

As she came undone beneath him, Chris offered up a satisfied smile. His green eyes, usually so playful and mischievous, now blazed with a feral intensity. He didn't slow, didn't pause to let her catch her breath; instead, he continued thrusting, chasing his own release. "Haven't come yet," he panted, the smirk that had charmed countless others now a promise of pleasures yet to unfurl.

Chapter 12

The rhythmic pounding merged with the creaks of the bed frame as it struck the wall in time with Chris's thrusts. Kira, beneath him, was lost in a haze of raw sensation and fragmented sobs, her body shaking under the onslaught of pleasure that ripped through her again and again. As she crested the wave of her fourth climax, a guttural cry escaped her lips, mingling with Chris's own grunt of release.

He collapsed momentarily beside her, then peeled off the used condom with a practiced motion, tossing it into the bin with an audible plop. His hand reached towards the nightstand for another, but Kira's fingers wrapped around his wrist, still trembling. "You win," she gasped out, chest heaving, her voice a threadbare whisper of surrender.

Chris's response was a smile, the corners of his mouth twitching upwards as he remembered the playful wager they'd set earlier that evening. The one where she'd defiantly claimed she could outlast him. His chuckle was low and warm, filled with satisfaction not just from their physical escapades but the victory over her stubborn resistance.

He glanced down at her, at the intimate place still pulsing from their fiery joining. Rising to his feet, he slipped into his jeans, the fabric brushing against his still-erect member, a testament to his enduring arousal. In the confines of the small bathroom, he ran the tap until the water was pleasantly warm before soaking a towel.

Returning to Kira, Chris knelt by the bed, his movements tender as he cleaned the evidence of their coupling from her skin. She watched him, eyes heavy-lidded yet sharp, tracking his every move.

"How?" she murmured, gaze flickering down to his unabated hardness.

"High libido," he said with a grin, running the cloth along her inner thigh, "and a lot of stamina." His smile widened, teasing. "Dangerous mix."

Kira could only nod, her mind still foggy with afterglow. But as she caught sight of the darkness that had settled outside the window, reality began to seep back in. She pushed herself up, her muscles protesting faintly, and reached for her clothes scattered haphazardly on the floor.

"I should go," she stated, the words sounding far more resolute than she felt. Her hands fumbled with her blouse, attempting to regain some semblance of the composed woman who had walked into this room hours before.

Kira's breath hitched as Chris's solid frame trapped her against the cool wall, his green eyes locked onto hers with a playful yet predatory glint. His chest heaved slightly from their earlier exertions, yet there was an undeniable edge of control in his posture, a silent demand that she acknowledge something she'd much rather leave unsaid.

"Say it, Kira," he murmured, voice low and dangerously smooth. "Before you go."

The rapid thumping of her heart filled her ears. Despite her mind's foggy resistance, her body betrayed her with its sensitivity to his proximity. She groaned, a sound of frustration, and rolled her eyes in an attempt to deflect the intensity of the moment.

"I can't handle you, there. Are you happy?" The words spilled out, laced with reluctant admission and a tired exasperation.

Chris's response was a simple, smug smile as he stepped back, creating space between them. "Very," he replied, watching her with satisfaction.

Kira quickly gathered her scattered belongings, her movements still unsteady. As she slung her bag over her shoulder, Chris's offer came unexpectedly, softening the charged atmosphere that lingered between them.

"Let me drive you home."

Surprised by the gesture and the fleeting glimpse of consideration behind his usual bravado, Kira paused, then nodded. "Thanks," she said, accepting the truce and the ride back to the safety of her own world.

Chapter 13

Monday morning rolled around, and Chris Morin was in a damn good mood.

He walked into class whistling, his usual swagger turned up a notch. The past few days had been interesting, to say the least. His test had gone well, he'd had a great time at the club, and—most importantly—he and Kira fucked.

And he hadn't stopped thinking about it.

As he dropped into his seat, stretching out his legs in front of him, a classmate, Mark, leaned over with a smirk.

"Damn, Morin, you're in a good mood. What, you finally got yourself a girlfriend?"

Chris furrowed his brows, turning to him. "What the hell are you talking about?"

Mark laughed. "Dude, David's been telling everyone about the girl you were at the club with. Says you two were looking real cozy."

Chris exhaled sharply, shaking his head. "David needs to shut the hell up."

Mark raised an eyebrow. "So it's true? You got a thing going on with this girl?"

Chris scoffed. "No. She's just my tutor."

Mark gave him a look. "Right. And you bring all your tutors to the club?"

Chris rolled his eyes. "It wasn't like that."

Mark shrugged, clearly unconvinced. "Whatever you say, man. But everyone's talking. Guess you're off the market."

Chris snorted. "I'm not off the market. I don't do relationships, and I definitely don't have time for a girlfriend."

Mark smirked. "Uh-huh. Tell that to the girl you took out on a Saturday night."

Chris didn't bother replying. He just shook his head, leaning back in his chair.

Kira Adams was not his girlfriend.

And he definitely, definitely didn't want one.

Right?

Chapter 14

hris refreshed the webpage again, even though he already knew what it said.

His grades were going up.

He leaned back against his headboard, a rare sense of pride settling in. He wasn't just scraping by, he was actually improving. And he knew exactly who to thank for that.

Grinning, he grabbed his phone and shot off a text.

Chris: *Guess who just checked his grades and is officially a genius?*

It didn't take long for Kira to reply.

Kira: *Oh, so I tutored Einstein this whole time?*

Chris: *Basically. But seriously, my grades are going up. You did good, Teach.*

Kira: *Proud of you.*

Something about those words made his chest feel too warm, so he ignored it and typed quickly before he thought too much about it.

Chris: *You should come to my game Friday. Consider it a reward for all your hard work.*

Kira: *That doesn't sound like a reward. That sounds like loud crowds and overpriced stadium food.*

Chris smirked.

Chris: *And yet... you didn't say no.*

Three dots appeared. Then disappeared. Then appeared again.

Kira: *Fine. I'll come.*

Chris grinned, tossing his phone on the bed.

Friday night came and the stadium was packed.

Kira sat in the stands, arms crossed as she took in the scene around her—cheerleaders hyping up the crowd, fans waving signs, and a sea of people wearing the school's colors. She wasn't the type to get excited over sports, but there was something electric about the energy in the stadium.

Then the team ran onto the field.

The crowd roared, and Kira's eyes immediately found him.

Chris looked different out there—focused, intense, every movement purposeful as he adjusted his gloves and settled into position. His usual cocky grin was replaced with something sharper, more determined.

The game started, and to Kira's own shock, she found herself watching with genuine interest.

Chris was fast.

Every time he took off down the field, the defenders barely kept up. He dodged, weaved, jumped over one guy entirely, and caught a deep pass with an ease that made it look effortless.

Kira barely realized she was holding her breath until the crowd erupted into cheers when Chris scored a touchdown.

Without thinking, she shot to her feet, cheering along with everyone else.

As the team celebrated on the field, Chris turned his head, scanning the stands—until his eyes landed on her.

For a second, the chaos of the game faded.

A slow, knowing smirk stretched across his face. He lifted two fingers to his temple in a salute, like he'd expected her to be watching.

Kira felt her entire body warm.

She quickly sat back down, clearing her throat.

She was just here to support her student. That was all.

But as the game continued, she couldn't help but watch him.

And she couldn't help but smile.

Chapter 15

Chris barely stepped out of the locker room before pulling out his phone. His muscles ached, but it was the good kind of sore, the kind that came with a hard-fought win. The game had been electric, but what stuck in his mind more than anything was the moment he'd looked up and seen her.

Kira Adams, standing in the stands, cheering for him.

He smirked to himself as he typed out a text.

Chris: *You looked like you were actually enjoying yourself tonight, Kira.*

A few moments later, his phone buzzed.

Kira: *I was. Shockingly.*

Chris chuckled.

Chris: *Told you football's not so bad.*

Kira: *Don't get carried away.*

Chris shook his head, still grinning.

Chris: *Come celebrate with me tomorrow. My place.*

The three dots appeared, then disappeared, then appeared again.

Kira: *Do I have to?*

Chris: *Yes. Consider it part of your tutoring contract.*

After a long pause, her reply came through.

Kira: *Fine. But if this turns into some frat boy party, I'm leaving.*

Chris: *Noted. See you tomorrow, Teach.*

He slipped his phone into his pocket, still in a ridiculously good mood, when he heard his name.

"Chris!"

He turned to see Molly Hayes leaning against the wall, arms crossed, her blonde waves perfectly styled despite the late hour. Her blue eyes raked over him with familiarity, like she still had some kind of claim to him.

"Hey, Molly," he said, already knowing where this was going.

She stepped closer, her perfume too strong, too intentional. "Hell of a game tonight," she purred. "Thought we could celebrate. My place?"

Chris exhaled, shaking his head. "Can't. Got other plans."

Molly's smile faltered slightly. "Oh?"

"Yeah," he said simply. Then, without another word, he turned and walked away.

Molly stiffened, her nails digging into her palm.

A second later, David strolled out of the locker room, stretching his arms over his head. He barely made it a few steps before Molly grabbed his arm.

"What the hell is up with him lately?" she demanded.

David raised an eyebrow. "Who, Morin?"

"Yes," she snapped, glaring at the spot Chris had just been standing. "He's been... different."

David smirked. "Yeah. He's got a new girlfriend."

Molly's expression froze.

Then she slowly turned back to where Chris had disappeared down the hallway, a deep frown settling on her face.

Chapter 16

Chris's grin spread across his face as Kira walked into the room, her gaze immediately drawn to the feast laid out on his table. Rows of white cartons, their sides glistening with condensation from the warm contents within, promised a culinary indulgence.

"Did you order all this?" she asked incredulously, eyes wide as she took in the mountain of shrimp fried rice and orange chicken.

"Guilty as charged," Chris chuckled, sliding a box toward her. "I've got a big appetite."

Kira shook her head, amusement dancing in her deep brown eyes. "It's enough to feed an entire football team."

"Or just one very hungry one," he quipped, scooping a generous portion onto his plate.

They settled on the couch, the movie starting up on the screen before them. As they dug into the takeout, Kira's focus seemed split between the cheesy romantic comedy she'd picked and the flavors of the food. Chris couldn't help but tease her about her film choice.

"Seriously, why do you like these movies? They're so…" He raised an eyebrow, watching her for a reaction.

"Exactly," Kira replied confidently. "They're good."

"Good and unrealistic are two different things," he countered playfully. "Like, who actually runs through an airport to stop someone from getting on a plane?"

Her laughter echoed in the room, a sound that lightened the air around them.

As the movie progressed, the predictable plot led to the inevitable reconciliation of the central couple. They kissed on screen, and Kira's smile turned soft, her attention fixed on the lovers' embrace. Chris watched her, not the actors, noting the way the corners of her mouth lifted in a contented curve.

"Come on, that's terrible kissing," he muttered, nudging her gently with his elbow.

"Really?" Kira turned to him, her challenge clear. "Think you could do better?"

"Absolutely," Chris said, confidence lacing his voice. Without hesitating, he reached out, tilting her chin upward and capturing her lips with his own.

The kiss was brief, but when he pulled away, he found Kira staring back at him with a dazed, almost dreamy expression. A smirk played on his lips as he leaned in closer, barely a breath away from her ear.

"Admit it, you're an amateur," he whispered.

Kira's response was immediate. She gasped, pulling back slightly. "Amateur? I am not!"

Chris let out a hearty laugh, the sound rich and inviting. "You kiss like a fish," he teased, poking at her pride.

"Excuse me?" Her tone was playful but laced with mock offense, and they shared a moment of laughter, the sound mingling with the dialogue from the cheesy movie neither of them were watching anymore.

Chris leaned back, a self-assured grin tugging at the corners of his mouth as he settled against the plush armrest of the couch. His green eyes held a playful glint that was nearly as mischievous as the challenge he laid before her. "Give it another shot," he said, voice low and inviting. "I'll give you a chance to redeem yourself."

With a mix of determination and a hint of hesitation, Kira moved to straddle him, her knees sinking into the cushions on either side of his thighs. She hesitated for only a fraction of a second before leaning down to press her lips to his in a kiss that was anything but amateur. It was a slow, deliberate connection, sensuality weaving through each movement like a silent promise.

Chris responded instinctively, his arms encircling her waist to pull her closer, deepening the kiss. The subtlety of their movements spoke volumes more than any words could, eloquently expressing the growing heat between them. As her lips moved against his with newfound confidence, a moan vibrated from his chest into the space where their mouths met.

His hands roamed lower, fingertips tracing the curve of her hips before gripping firmly, squeezing in a way that elicited a soft whimper from her. The sound, so vulnerable and genuine, broke through the haze that had settled over Kira's mind, cutting the ties of the momentary spell she'd been under.

Abruptly, she pulled away, breaking the kiss and planting her hands on his chest as if to steady herself. Her breath came in shallow gasps, betraying the internal struggle that flickered across her features. "I... I should go," she stammered, her voice barely above a whisper.

But Chris wasn't ready to let the night end—not when every fiber of his being was attuned to the woman above him. He reached up, his hand slipping beneath the hem of her skirt with a boldness only he could muster. His fingers found the warmth and wetness there, evidence of her desire.

"I think you should stay," he murmured, the words laced with a mixture of command and entreaty. The look in his eyes dared her to deny what they both felt, the intensity of the moment hanging heavy in the air between them.

Chapter 17

Chris' relentless devotion to Kira's pleasure had her world tilting on its axis, his head a fervent worshipper beneath the altar of her skirt. Her breath hitched, body tensing as waves of ecstasy crashed over her. The fabric of her blouse clung to her skin with the intensity of their encounter, her fingers clawing at the air as if trying to anchor herself in the storm of sensation he elicited. Even as she reached the peak, her climax hitting her like a freight train, Chris didn't relent. His tongue continued its dance, pushing her into spasms that made her entire frame shudder.

"Chris... please," she gasped out, the words barely a whisper among her moans, "it's too much." Her plea, edged with desperation, finally pierced through his haze of desire. With a final, lingering kiss to her trembling clit, he pulled away, sitting back on his heels. His lips glistened, a testament to her unraveling, and he swiped his tongue across them with a satisfied grin.

Kira's gaze drifted downwards, catching sight of the prominent bulge straining against his pajama pants. A switch flipped inside her; the woman who could cut through anyone's nonsense was now navigating uncharted waters, her usual confidence replaced by an anticipatory nervousness. Her hand reached out, hesitating for only a heartbeat before contacting the hard ridge of his erection. Through the thin cotton, she felt him, alive, pulsing and her touch coerced a deep, primal moan from his chest.

"Want to touch it?" Chris breathed, his voice roughened with need, eyes darkening with a challenge she couldn't resist.

She nodded, her throat dry, and watched as he discarded his pants with one swift motion. Her hand enveloped his length, the heat and weight of him sending a jolt of electricity down her spine. Chris responded instantly, grinding into her palm, his precum slick at the tip, a silent promise of what was to come.

"I need to be inside you," he declared, urgency lacing every syllable. It wasn't a question, but the offer of a connection deeper than any tutoring session or verbal spar they'd ever shared.

Locking eyes with him, Kira saw not just the cocky football player, but the man who challenged her every notion of control and professionalism. And in that moment, her decision was made. She gave a single, determined nod, surrendering to the intense current pulling her under.

Chris, propelled by a hunger that had been building between them for days, swept Kira up in his arms with an ease that spoke of his strength and athletic prowess. The air seemed to crackle with the electric charge of their connection as he maneuvered through the hallway, her body pressed tightly against his. He entered his bedroom, a place marked by scattered football memorabilia and the faint scent of cologne, and laid her gently on the rumpled bedding.

Without hesitation, Chris peeled off his shirt, revealing the chiseled contours of his chest and abdomen — every muscle a testament to his discipline and athleticism. His green eyes locked onto Kira's with a fiery intensity as he reached for a condom, his movements swift and practiced. Climbing onto the bed, he admired Kira's curves, her dark curls fanned out on the pillow, and her deep brown eyes, usually so sharp and discerning, now clouded with desire.

He positioned himself between her legs, which she willingly parted, inviting him in. As he entered her slowly, the depth of his longing was mirrored in each careful inch he moved forward. Kira's breath hitched, her petite frame tensing beneath him, and Chris paused, his voice a low hiss urging her to let go of her restraint. "Relax," he instructed, a flare of concern cutting through the fog of his lust.

"Chris… you're too big," Kira whimpered, a mix of awe and trepidation in her voice. Her words struck a chord in him, reminding him that despite his usual confidence, he wanted this to be good for her, not just another conquest.

In response, he lifted her shirt, exposing the soft mounds of her breasts. Leaning down, he enveloped one nipple with his mouth, the sensation drawing a sharp cry from her that echoed off the walls. She arched into him, her back forming a perfect bow, and as she relaxed, he seized the moment to drive himself fully into her. Her second cry was louder, filled with a complex melody of pain and pleasure.

Driven by her sounds and responses, Chris found a rhythm, thrusting into her with a growing fervor. Each movement was a silent promise to fulfill the desire they both felt. He glanced down to witness their union, the sight of his cock, glistening with her arousal, disappearing inside her again and again.

"So wet," he moaned, the raw honesty of the moment stripping away his usual playful bravado.

Kira's reply was unintelligible, her voice lost in the waves of sensation. "Deep…so deep," she managed to utter between labored breaths.

"Yeah? You like it deep?" Chris asked, a surge of primal satisfaction flooding him at her nod. His mischievous glint transformed into something more carnal, a side of him that few women ever truly saw.

"I'll go as deep as you want," he vowed, lifting himself into a new position that allowed him to deliver on his word. With each powerful thrust, he sought to reach the places within her that had never been touched, to claim a victory far different than those won on the football field.

This joining was not a game, and as he watched Kira surrender beneath him, Chris realized that for the first time, he wasn't just chasing another score; he was seeking something deeper—a connection that might just break through his defenses and challenge the very essence of who he thought he was.

Chris's muscles tightened, and his movements became a testament to years of honed athletic prowess. He drove into her with a relentless rhythm, each stroke propelling them further into a maelstrom of pleasure. Kira's screams crescendoed under the pressure of his hand against her lips, muffling the sound that was music to his ears.

"You feel so good, Kira, fuck," Chris grunted, his voice a low growl vibrating through the charged air between them. His piercing green eyes locked onto hers, the intensity within them reflecting the depth of his desire.

Kira's hands were wild, clawing at the blanket beneath her, as if trying to anchor herself in the tempest of sensation he was stirring inside her. He hit that spot, that secret haven of nerve endings, over and over, each time like the first—unpredictable and shockingly sweet.

The room was filled with the sounds of their union, the slick slide of skin on skin, and the primal rhythm of bodies moving in sync. Chris felt the pull, the incredible tightening that heralded his own impending climax, but he held back, chasing the wave along with her until she crested first.

With a shuddering gasp, Kira's body tightened around him, her orgasm washing over her in a wave that left her breathless and quivering. Only then did Chris allow himself to follow, pouring every last ounce of himself into her with a series of deep, deliberate thrusts that left him spent and reeling.

As they both panted, coming back down from the dizzying heights, Chris gently removed his hand from her mouth and replaced it with his lips, kissing her softly. It was a kiss unlike any other—a silent promise that what had just transpired between them was more than a mere physical release; it was the beginning of an uncharted journey neither of them had planned for.

Chapter 18

Kira's fingers clawed at the sheets, her arm stretching forward in a desperate attempt to find something to anchor to as Chris yanked her away from the headboard. His grip was iron on her wrist, his laughter a low rumble as he drove into her with a force that made her entire body quiver. The relentless rhythm sent the headboard crashing against the wall in a rhythmic beat.

"Ah—don't give up on me now," he teased, breath hot against her ear.

Kira could only gasp, her lungs fighting for air as sweat slicked her skin. Every thrust pinned her harder against him, and she felt owned by the intensity of it all. She couldn't have pulled away even if she wanted to; the pleasure was merciless, overwhelming.

"Look at you, taking my cock better than ever," Chris hissed with unbridled lust, his gaze burning over her trembling form. "Fuck, I love the way you suck me back in when I try to pull out."

Underneath him, Kira lay panting, her mind a haze of delirium. Drool spilled unchecked from the corner of her mouth as he continued his savage pace, her world reduced to the singular sensation of being filled completely, relentlessly.

Their fucking had turned the bed into a wasteland of latex—a testament to their hours spent entwined. As Chris hit that divine spot inside her once more, stars exploded behind Kira's eyes, and her voice broke into a plea, though her pride fought to silence it. "Ple-please, I'm so close," she whispered, her words barely coherent.

His response was a smile that she could feel rather than see, his breath ragged with exertion as he murmured into her ear. "Yeah? You want me to go deep again?" he asked, his tone playful yet demanding.

Kira could only nod, her whole body trembling on the edge of oblivion. But Chris was not satisfied with silence.

"No," he commanded, his voice a growl of desire. "I want to hear you beg for it."

Kira's voice trembled, a mix of desperation and desire cracking through the words that spilled from her lips. "Pl-please, I wa-want it deeper, I want to come," she gasped, her plea mingling with the sounds of skin slapping against skin.

Chris's response was a low chuckle, his lips parting to reveal the hint of a predatory smile. "That's my girl," he praised her, his green eyes gleaming with triumph. His hands shifted, iron grips seizing her hips and anchoring her firmly against the mattress. With a powerful thrust, he plunged into her depths, eliciting a scream that pierced the room's heavy air.

"Shh…Don't want the neighbors to come knocking, do we?" Chris's voice was a husky whisper as he pressed his palm over her mouth, smothering the sounds of her ecstasy. Beneath his hand, Kira's muffled cries vibrated, her body writhing in a silent symphony of pleasure and torment.

The moment unfurled like a tempest within her, the build-up reaching its crescendo. Then, abruptly, an orgasm tore through Kira's core, a force so intense it robbed her of breath and strength. She stiffened beneath him as the wave crashed down, leaving her to collapse onto the sweat-soaked sheets with a sound swallowed by Chris's hand.

He turned her over onto her back. Hovering above her, Chris watched the aftermath, a mixture of awe and lust swirling in his chest. Her dazed expression drew a chuckle from him, a low rumble vibrating through his chest. "Shit, you're out of it," he murmured, almost to himself.

He repositioned himself, teasing her entrance with the tip of his cock, swollen and eager. With deliberate slowness, he sank back inside her, savoring the way her inner muscles greeted him. Pressing his athletic frame flush against hers, he resumed thrusting, pounding into her with renewed frenzy.

Her nails found his back, carving pathways of red that only fueled his desire. Despite the sting, he didn't falter; instead, he welcomed the pain mixed with pleasure. Her walls clenched around him like a silken vice, drawing a groan from his throat. "You feel so fucking good, Kira," he grunted, each word punctuated by the rhythm of their bodies colliding in the dimly lit room.

Chris's breaths were ragged, the scent of her skin intoxicating as he buried his head into the crook of Kira's neck. His lips found her pulse point, sucking gently, and she gasped out loud—a sound that echoed the pounding of her heart. With a calculated thrust that went deeper, he hit that sweet spot inside her, watching as another climax shattered her poise, her body shaking beneath him.

"Fuck, Chris..." Her voice was a breathy whisper, trailing off into silence as she came undone.

His own release was close on her heels, a groan tearing from his throat as he spilled into the condom, the sensation overwhelming. He lingered for a moment, reveling in the aftershocks that rippled through her before he gently withdrew.

"Kira," Chris murmured, peeling off the used protection and tossing it with a soft plop into the waste bin. He couldn't help but whistle lowly at the sight of their spent passion, condoms littered like trophies of their lust and sheets dampened. Leaning over to kiss her trembling lips, he whispered praise into her mouth, "That was so fucking good, Kira."

Her laugh was weak, a tender acknowledgment of their shared satisfaction. Pulling back, he checked the time on his phone, the numbers glaring back at him. 3:00 AM. A sigh escaped him as he muttered, "It's late. Stay the night."

She glanced at the clock on his phone, nodding in agreement. The idea of navigating home at this hour seemed ludicrous. "Yeah, I'm not going anywhere," she conceded, her voice still laced with the remnants of exhaustion.

"The shower's yours if you need it," he offered, watching her struggle to find her strength.

"Too weak," she breathed out, the words tinged with contentment and fatigue.

A chuckle bubbled up from his chest as he lifted her effortlessly into his arms, carrying her towards the bathroom where he started the shower. The sound of water cascading down filled the room while Chris fetched a towel from the closet. Helping Kira step inside the warm embrace of the steam, he didn't miss the surprised flicker in her eyes when he joined her under the spray.

As they washed away the evidence of their indulgence, Kira felt the firm press of his arousal against her back, a silent testament to his insatiable desire. "If we do this again, I won't be able to walk tomorrow," she half-joked, half-warned, leaning into the touch of his lips on her shoulder.

"I understand," he murmured, his voice a soothing balm as they finished rinsing off. After stepping out of the shower, Chris handed her one of his t-shirts. It smelled like him—a mixture of cologne and something uniquely

Chris.

While she dressed, he swiftly changed the bed linens, erasing the chaos of their previous encounters. They settled into the fresh sheets, bodies drawing close, seeking the comfort of each other's warmth. Wrapped in an intimate cuddle, the world outside their cocoon ceased to exist, and soon, deep sleep claimed them both, their breaths syncing in the quiet aftermath of the storm.

Chapter 19

Kira stared blankly at her notebook, pen hovering above the page, her mind miles away from the lecture.

She was supposed to be taking notes, supposed to be paying attention, but instead, all she could think about was Chris Morin.

The way his hands had gripped her waist. The heat of his breath against her skin. The way his lips had moved against hers, slow at first, then deeper, more demanding.

Her body flushed at the memory.

Oh God.

She snapped out of it, her eyes widening as she shifted in her seat and cleared her throat. She needed to focus.

Kira quickly scribbled down the last thing the professor said, forcing herself back into the moment. But it didn't last.

Her mind drifted again, her thoughts tangled in him, his teasing smirk, his lazy confidence, the way he always found a way to get under her skin, and worse—how much she secretly liked it.

This was dangerous territory.

The sound of students shuffling their things snapped her back to reality, and she let out a quiet breath.

Class was over.

Thank God. She packed up her stuff and left, trying to push Chris from her mind. But as she stepped outside and started toward home, a familiar voice stopped her.

"Kira!"

She turned and saw Chris leaning casually against a wall, looking as annoyingly handsome as ever in a fitted T-shirt and jeans. His green eyes glinted with something playful as he smirked at her.

Kira's lips twitched. "What are you doing here?"

Chris shrugged. "Figured you might be hungry. Let's grab lunch."

Kira raised an eyebrow. "So now you're inviting me to things?"

Chris grinned. "What can I say? You're growing on me."

She rolled her eyes but couldn't hide the small smile creeping onto her lips. "Fine. But I'm picking the place."

Chris smirked. "Deal."

As they made their way through the parking lot toward his car, Kira was starting to enjoy this. That is, until—

"Chris!"

They both turned toward the voice.

Molly.

She approached with a perfectly practiced smile, her blonde hair shiny and flawless, her body language all too confident. She looked Chris up and down before stopping just close enough to be too close.

"Hey," she said sweetly, her blue eyes flicking between them. "Didn't see you after the game."

Chris gave her a neutral nod. "Yeah, been busy."

Molly pouted slightly. "You planning on going to Matt's party this weekend?"

Chris shrugged. "I'll think about it."

Molly finally turned to Kira, her eyes scanning her up and down with barely concealed curiosity.

"You must be Kira," she said, tilting her head. "I'm Molly Hayes. Head cheerleader and Chris' ex."

Kira didn't flinch, didn't even blink—but she could feel the undercurrent of malice behind those words.

Chris, however, let out a quiet sigh, already annoyed.

Kira smiled, unfazed. "Nice to meet you."

Molly's lips curled. "You should come to the party too. It'll be fun."

Chris immediately cut in. "Yeah, that's not really Kira's scene."

Molly's eyes flickered with something unreadable, but her smile didn't waver.

Kira, sensing the tension, smiled politely. "Thanks for the invite, though."

Molly nodded, but there was something sharp in her expression, something that said this wasn't over.

Chris didn't give her the chance to say anything else. "Alright, we gotta go," he said smoothly, guiding Kira toward his car with a hand on her lower back.

As they climbed inside and Chris pulled out of the parking lot, neither of them noticed Molly watching them, her fingers tightening around the strap of her purse, her smile long gone.

She turned on her heel, her jaw clenched.

Kira sat at her desk, surrounded by textbooks and highlighted notes, her laptop open to a study guide. The upcoming test was important, and she was determined to ace it.

She had everything she needed, her planner, her flashcards, a fresh cup of coffee. She was in total focus mode.

Her phone buzzed once. Then again. Then again.

A flood of notifications lit up her screen.

Chris.

She sighed, shaking her head. What does he want now?

Opening the messages, she was immediately greeted by an aggressive rant.

Chris: *What the actual hell is this?*

Chris: *I put on some rom-com, and this dude just drove through a tornado warning. Like, why? He could've just CALLED.*

Chris: *Oh, great. Now they're breaking up.*

Chris: *Oh, WAIT. I bet you ten bucks they'll get back together in the last five minutes.*

Kira smirked, already amused.

Kira: *Why are you watching a rom-com?*

A response came instantly.

Chris: *Nothing else was on.*

Kira laughed, shaking her head.

Kira: *Liar. You totally picked it on purpose.*

Chris: *Okay, maybe. But these lines are killing me, Kira. This guy just said, "You're the only thing that's ever made sense in my life."*

Chris: *WHAT DOES THAT EVEN MEAN?*

Kira burst out laughing, covering her mouth so she wouldn't wake her roommate.

Kira: *It means he loves her, you idiot.*

Chris: *Yeah? Well, maybe he should've figured that out BEFORE he let her walk out dramatically in the rain.*

Kira's heart fluttered at his texts, at the fact that he was sharing this moment with her, even through a screen.

Chris: *Oh, wait. Here it is. The big grand gesture.*

Chris: *I KNEW IT. THEY'RE BACK TOGETHER. THIS IS SO PREDICTABLE.*

Chris: *...Kinda satisfying, though.*

Kira stared at that last message, something warm and unexpected curling in her chest.

She typed back quickly.

Kira: *So what you're saying is... you liked it.*

A pause.

Chris: *No comment.*

Kira smiled, staring at the screen longer than she should have, rereading their messages, feeling that feeling growing inside her.

Then, it hit her.

She liked Chris Morin.

Not just in a he's fun to be around way. Not just in a he's a good distraction way.

In a real way.

And suddenly, she wasn't sure what to do with that.

Chapter 20

The sun beat down on the field as Chris wiped sweat from his brow, catching his breath between drills. Practice had been brutal, but nothing he couldn't handle.

David and Malik jogged over, grinning like they were about to start trouble.

"So," David started, stretching his arms behind his head, "how's life with the new girlfriend?"

Chris gave him a deadpan look. "She's not my girlfriend."

Malik snorted. "Yeah, okay."

David shook his head. "Nah, man. We're not buying it. You never keep a girl around this long—except Molly."

As if summoned, Molly Hayes who was practicing with her squad nearby, sauntered over, tossing her blonde hair over her shoulder. "Talking about me?" she asked sweetly.

Chris sighed. "Not really."

Undeterred, she turned to David and Malik. "What are we talking about?"

"Matt's party," David said, turning back to Chris. "You coming?"

Chris shrugged. "Nah. Parties aren't Kira's thing."

Silence.

Chris looked up to find both of his teammates staring at him, smirking like they'd just caught him red-handed.

He frowned. "What?"

David chuckled. "We didn't say anything about Kira."

Malik grinned. "We asked if *you* were going."

Chris opened his mouth, then closed it, realization sinking in.

Damn it.

David clapped him on the back. "Just admit it, man. Say the words, and we'll leave you alone."

Chris exhaled. "She's not my girlfriend."

Molly, who had been watching all of this very closely, suddenly smirked. "Then prove it."

Chris arched a brow. "What?"

She crossed her arms. "Come to the party. You know, have a little fun. Unless, of course, you're busy?"

Chris felt three pairs of eyes locked on him, waiting.

He sighed. "Fine. I'll go."

David and Malik exchanged victorious looks, and Molly's smirk widened.

Chris suddenly had a bad feeling about this.

Chapter 21

Kira gathered her things and slung her bag over her shoulder, ready to leave after a long day of classes. She had barely stepped into the hallway when a too-sweet voice stopped her.

"Kira!"

She turned and found Molly Hayes standing there, looking effortlessly put together, as if she hadn't just been lurking outside the classroom, waiting for her.

Kira raised a brow. "Molly."

Molly flashed her signature perfectly rehearsed smile. "I just wanted to let you know that Chris decided last minute to come to Matt's party tonight." She tilted her head, watching for Kira's reaction. "So... you should come too."

Kira hesitated. "I don't really do parties."

Molly waved a dismissive hand. "Oh, come on, it'll be fun! Plus, you wouldn't want Chris to be all alone with a bunch of drunk cheerleaders, would you?"

Kira stiffened at the not-so-subtle implication.

She didn't like the way Molly was looking at her, like she was waiting for her to react, waiting for her to admit something.

So, against her better judgment, she exhaled and said, "Fine. I'll go."

Molly's smile widened, a little too pleased. "Great. See you there, tutor."

With that, she turned on her heel and disappeared down the hallway.

Kira sighed, already regretting this.

Dressed in a short yellow dress that hugged her curves and a pair of wedges, Kira stepped out of the cab in front of the party.

The house was packed. Music thumped from inside, shaking the walls, and people spilled onto the front lawn, laughing and talking loudly.

She hesitated for half a second before squaring her shoulders. Pushing through the crowd, she made her way inside, scanning the sea of faces.

Then she heard him.

Coming from the kitchen.

"For the last time, she isn't my girlfriend."

Kira slowed her steps, heart skipping a beat. She moved closer to the doorway, just out of sight, listening.

Chris was in the kitchen, surrounded by his teammates, drink in hand, looking frustrated but amused as his friends laughed.

"Yeah, yeah, pretty boy, keep telling yourself that," Malik teased.

Chris rolled his eyes, taking a sip of his drink.

Kira frowned, shifting on her feet. She didn't know why she was standing there, didn't know why she felt the need to hear what he'd say next.

"We told you to prove it," David added.

Chris sighed. "I'm here, aren't I?"

"That's not enough," Malik smirked. "Listen, Molly is outside in the pool, in the tiniest bikini I've ever seen." The room erupted into laughter.

Kira's stomach dropped.

"Prove to us you're single and go make out with her," Malik continued.

Chris let out a frustrated sigh, rubbing a hand down his face. "Is that what will get you off my back?"

His teammates whooped in response.

Chris groaned. "Fine."

Chapter 22

Chris led his teammates through the sliding glass doors, spilling into Matt's expansive backyard where the setting sun cast a golden hue over the scene. The air buzzed with the chatter of cheerleaders lounging in the azure pool, their laughter echoing like a siren's song.

"Morin!" Malik's voice cut through the din as he gestured to Molly Hayes, emerging from the water like some mythic nymph, droplets cascading down her toned limbs. Chris's gaze lingered on her for a moment, she was an image of calculated perfection.

As Molly strutted toward them, the crowd formed a tight circle, their eyes gleaming with anticipation. "Prove it," they began to chant, each repetition more insistent than the last. The pressure mounted around Chris like a vice.

With a resigned sigh that betrayed his turmoil, Chris reached out, pulling Molly close. His lips met hers in a kiss charged with a sensuality that contradict his internal resistance. She reciprocated, wrapping her arms around his neck, her fingers tangling in his tousled hair. The throng erupted into cheers and whistles, but their jubilation fell on deaf ears as Chris pulled away, searching their faces.

"Happy now?" he demanded, a hint of bitterness seeping into his tone. Yet, even as he spoke, an inexplicable wave of emptiness surged within him—a longing for something genuine.

Pivoting on his heel, Chris stalked towards the house, desperate to escape the suffocating charade. But the moment his feet hit the patio stones, his green eyes locked with Kira's deep brown stare across the yard. Her expression was unreadable, cold as ice, yet beneath the surface, a flicker of hurt betrayed her indifference.

"Kira…" he started, but she turned sharply, her curls bouncing with each determined step as she distanced herself from the spectacle.

"Damn it," Chris cursed under his breath, the uncharacteristic edge of desperation to his voice spurring him into action. He took off after her, every muscle in his athletic frame propelling him forward, driven by a need to explain, to apologize—to salvage whatever fragment of respect might still exist between them.

Chris chased the echo of her name down the sidewalk, his voice a rough plea against the evening air. "Kira!" But she was a retreating shadow, her pace unyielding, as if each step could distance her from what she'd witnessed.

"Wait up," he insisted, catching up to her with a few long strides honed on the football field. His hand reached out, fingers closing around her wrist with an unintentional firmness of desperation.

"Let me explain, it wasn't—"

"Save it," Kira cut him off, her voice sharp like the crack of a whip, yet she didn't pull away. Instead, she turned, her eyes two dark orbs reflecting a cold fire. Hurt shone through the ice, piercing him more acutely than any defender's tackle ever could. "It was just a kiss,"

"Chris, it was just a kiss?" She gave a hollow laugh that scraped at his insides, and her hand rose to cup her own face in disbelief. "Just a kiss? So you just go around kissing all your exes?"

78

Her question stung, needling at his conscience. He sighed, the weight of his teammates' expectations suddenly feeling like chains around his neck. "I... I just wanted to get the guys off my back, you know how it is."

She shook her head, curls swaying with the movement, disappointment etched into the fine lines of her face. "That's not good enough, Chris."

"Good enough?" He echoed, frustration creeping into his tone. A second sigh escaped him, heavier, full with an admission he hadn't planned to make. "What do you want from me, Kira? It's not like we were dating, we just fucked a few times."

The words hung between them, crass and ugly, and Kira's reaction was immediate. She gasped, her body recoiling as if struck, and when she faced him again, her brown eyes searched his green ones for something—anything—that might resemble the truth.

"Was that it? I was just a fuck...Truly?" Her voice cracked, revealing the fault lines of a heart he hadn't known he had the power to fracture.

Chris's mouth opened, but the space between them was suddenly vast and silent. Words failed him spectacularly, and all he could manage was a helpless shrug—a gesture that seemed to sever whatever tenuous connection remained.

Kira's posture went rigid, her slim form like a blade unsheathed and ready to cut ties with one swift motion. She blinked rapidly, and even from where he stood, Chris could see the sheen of unshed tears in her eyes, a testament to a pain he hadn't intended to inflict. Without a word, she turned on her heel, her movements brimming with a grace that didn't show the turmoil surely churning within her.

Rooted to the spot, Chris watched as Kira's retreating figure dwindled with every determined step. A rush of something—regret, anger, confusion—surged through his veins, finding release in a swift, violent arc as his foot lashed out at a nearby trash can. The metallic clang echoed down the street as the bin toppled and spilled its contents onto the concrete, a chaotic mess that mirrored the agitation inside him.

"Damn it," he cursed under his breath, the sound muffled by the thickening night air. His fingers threaded through his tousled hair, pulling at the strands as if to rid himself of the thoughts that now plagued him. His piercing green eyes, usually so sure and teasing, were clouded with a storm of emotions he couldn't name, let alone conquer.

Left alone in the wake of Kira's departure, Christopher Morin felt an unfamiliar hollowness—a void where his usual bravado failed to reach.

Chapter 23

Monday arrived, and Kira did what she did best—she focused. Or at least, she tried to.

She kept her eyes on her notes, her hands busy with assignments, and her thoughts locked firmly on school. But no matter how much she tried to drown herself in coursework, her mind betrayed her.

It drifted, back to Friday night, back to the party, back to the way her stomach had sunk when she'd seen him kiss Molly.

And worst of all? It drifted back to Chris himself. His stupid cocky smile, his teasing banter, the way he'd made her laugh, the way he'd made her feel.

She clenched her jaw and forced herself to push it all down.

When class ended, she quickly packed her things and left the building, determined to go home and move on with her day.

But then a voice called out to her.

"Kira!"

Her entire body tensed at the sound of his voice.

She turned her head just slightly and saw Chris, leaning against his car like he had all the time in the world. But the moment she met his eyes, he started moving—hurrying toward her, looking frustrated but determined.

Kira turned forward and kept walking.

"Seriously?" Chris scoffed, falling into step beside her. "You're just gonna ignore me?"

She said nothing, gripping the strap of her bag tighter.

Chris exhaled sharply. "Kira, come on. You can't just shut me out. I've been calling and texting you since Friday night."

"Yeah," she said flatly, still not slowing down. "And I didn't respond. That should tell you something."

Chris raked a hand through his hair. "Kira, we need to talk—"

"No, we don't."

He moved in front of her, forcing her to stop. "What are we supposed to do? You're my tutor, you can't just—"

Kira's eyes flashed, her voice like ice. "Get a new one."

Chris stilled, jaw tightening.

Then, without another word, she walked past him, leaving him standing alone, frustrated, speechless, and angry with himself.

Chapter 24

C hris slouched on the leather couch, his brooding gaze fixed on a
undistinguished spot on the opposite wall. The yelling and laughter
of the house party swirled around him like an irrelevant storm,
unable to shift the heavy cloud that had settled over him since Kira's silence
began. He hadn't heard from her in two weeks, not a text, not a call, and she
hadn't shown up at his last game. Chris searched the crowd for her face that
day, but it was like looking for a ghost.

"Man, have you ever seen Chris this down?" one teammate whispered to
another, their voices barely reaching above the music as they hovered nearby.

"Never. His head's not in the game either. Almost cost us big time last
Saturday," the other replied, shaking his head. There was concern etched
into their expressions, a rare sight when it came to their usually unflappable
friend.

As if summoned by the talk of his mood, a woman with a mischievous glint
in her eye slide up to Chris. She leaned close, her breath warm against his
ear. "Hey, why don't we go upstairs? Get away from this crowd."

Without a word, Chris flicked his half-empty cup onto the cluttered coffee
table, liquid splashing onto the wood surface carelessly. Rising to follow her
lead, he felt the weight of his own expectations pressing down on him. It
had been too long since he'd had sex - two weeks since he'd last touched or

been touched. But as they stumbled into the dimly lit bedroom, Chris told himself he deserved this release, deserved to feel something other than Kira's absence.

Their kissing was hungry, urgent, a frenzy of lips and teeth. But as her hand slipped beneath his waistband, a cold realization washed over him. There was no response from his body, no stirring of desire. Panic clawed at the edges of his mind.

Abruptly, Chris sat up, the world tilting slightly as he did so. "I can't do this. Sorry, another time," he muttered, his voice rough with confusion.

He straightened his clothes with jerky movements, fleeing the bedroom and the house without looking back. The calls of his friends faded behind him, meaningless noise compared to the deafening silence inside his car as he drove away, alone.

Chapter 25

C hris flopped onto his bed, the springs creaking under his weight. The blue glow of his phone screen illuminated his face as his thumb swiped upwards in a monotonous rhythm. Each video thumbnail blurred into the next, an indistinct parade of naked women and false ecstasy until one caught his attention—a thumbnail promising something different. He tapped it decisively.

The video buffered for a moment before playing, revealing a woman with brown skin that seemed to shimmer under the studio lights. Chris felt a jolt of recognition—the curve of her hips, the cascade of dark curls, they all echoed Kira's silhouette in his mind. He leaned back against the headboard, his breath catching slightly as he watched the woman move with an uncanny grace that was so reminiscent of Kira's fluid dance movements.

His hand drifted down, almost without thought, as if pulled by the magnetic force of the fantasy unfolding before him. Fingers wrapped around his growing arousal, a physical echo of the mental image that had lodged itself firmly in his head. Kira's deep brown eyes, warm yet piercing, and now somehow transposed onto the woman in the video. He began to stroke himself, feeling the heat and rigidity build with every imagined caress that he placed on Kira's flawless skin.

Chris' grip tightened, his breath hitched in short, rapid intakes as the woman on the screen reached her climax. Her moans, a sultry melody to the rhythm of his own hand spurred him on. "Oh fuck," he groaned into the dimness of his room, the sound more prayer than exclamation.

Each stroke was a chase, a pursuit of release that seemed to dance just out of reach until the fantasy before him peaked. The woman's back arched beautifully, a mirror to Kira's own passionate throws when she argued against his sassy remarks in their tutoring sessions. It was an image powerful enough to push him over the edge.

His eyelids fluttered shut, and for a fleeting moment, it wasn't the woman on the screen but Kira beneath his touch—her radiant brown skin flushed with pleasure, those sharp, deep brown eyes softened in ecstasy. The vision shattered as he climaxed, hot seed spilling through his fingers in a messy testament to his unsanctioned desire.

Panting, Chris opened his eyes to the afterglow on the screen, feeling the weight of realization settle heavily within him. He cursed under his breath, a mix of frustration and longing coloring the word as it left his lips. It wasn't the video, not the anonymous woman with her practiced performance. It was Kira, always Kira, who haunted his thoughts and now claimed dominion over his most intimate moments.

He could only get hard for Kira. The revelation stung, an unwanted truth that bound him to her in a way no amount of cocky charisma could undo. With a sigh, he wiped his hand with a tissue, the finality of his situation settling like dust in the silence of his room.

Chapter 26

Chris slammed his textbook shut, the echo bouncing off the lecture hall's walls as students turned to stare. His leg jittered like a jackhammer beneath the desk, muscles tensed with a raw, gnawing energy that had become all too familiar these past three weeks. The clock's second hand seemed to mock him, ticking away the seconds like a slow drip of water torturing the already parched.

"Excuse me," he muttered to no one in particular, shoving his way past knees and backpacks, ignoring the professor's bewildered pause mid-sentence. He burst through the doors, the afternoon sun glaring down as if to spotlight his hasty retreat.

His feet carried him swiftly across the campus green, each step fuelled by an insatiable frustration. Reaching his car, he fell into the driver's seat, the leather cool against his heated skin. A deep sigh escaped him, resonating within the confines of the vehicle as he leaned forward, resting his forehead on the steering wheel. His fingers fumbled for his phone, swiping it to life with a flicker of hope that quickly died, no messages from Kira. The emptiness of the screen felt like a punch to the gut. "Enough," he growled under his breath, tossing the device aside.

Nightfall found him outside her apartment building, heart drumming an erratic rhythm against his ribcage. The hallway was dimly lit and eerily silent, making his footsteps sound unnaturally loud as he approached her door.

When she swung it open, the light from inside spilled out, framing her silhouette. Her dark curls were loose, cascading over her shoulders, and her eyes held the surprised glint of someone caught off-guard. She blinked at him, then moves to close the door, as he wedged his foot in the doorway.

"Kira, just ten minutes, please," Chris implored, the words spilling out in a rush. There was a sigh, a quiet resignation as she reached back for her shoes, slipping them on with graceful precision. They walked together to his car, the silence between them heavy like a tangible thing.

Inside the car, the air felt charged as they settled into their seats. Chris took a moment, trying to gather the fragments of his thoughts. With a turn of his head, he faced her, but she was a statue beside him, arms crossed, her gaze fixed ahead.

"Kira... Look, I wanted to apologize. I'm sorry for being an asshole," he started, his voice unsteady as vulnerability clawed its way through his usual confidence. He watched her profile, the way her jaw clenched and unclenched, but she remained silent, unmoved.

"These last few weeks have been absolutely hell for me...I miss you, every day," he continued, the words feeling foreign yet necessary. It was like confessing to a priest, except the absolution he sought was far from guaranteed.

"I don't do relationships, they just aren't my thing," he admitted, the truth tasting bitter on his tongue. At this, she flinched, anger etched into the furrow of her brow, yet he pressed on. "After I kissed Molly at that party, I felt...guilty. And in some way... I think we were in a relationship. I was just too scared to put a label on it."

Her expression softened around the edges, an imperceptible shift that gave him the faintest glimmer of hope. He waited, his confession hanging in the air between them, charged with possibility.

The softening of Kira's eyes was subtle, like the melting of ice under a hesitant sun. She released a sigh that carried with it the weight of her defenses, and for a moment, the car felt less like a battleground and more like a confessional.

"And you were not just an easy fuck to me, Kira," Chris said, his voice low and rough around the edges. The words fell into the silence that had settled between them, each syllable heavy with meaning.

She turned her head, slowly, her gaze meeting his at last. There was a vulnerability in her deep brown eyes that he hadn't seen before, a tenderness that belied her usual armor of indifference. The sight of it sent a jolt through him, an electric flutter that started in his chest and spread outwards.

"There she is…" he whispered, almost to himself. In that look, in the slight uncurling of her arms from their defensive fold, he saw a glimpse of the Kira who he first met at the library, who loved corny rom-coms in these rare unguarded moments. It was as if he had been granted passage through the walls she so meticulously maintained.

Chris held her gaze, afraid to breathe too loudly, to shatter the fragile truce that seemed to be forming in the quiet of the car, under the dim glow of the streetlights outside. For now, the world narrowed down to this delicate connection, to the hope that flickered in the space between them.

Chapter 27

Chris shifted uncomfortably in the driver's seat, the leather sticking to his skin as Kira's penetrating gaze held him captive. "So let me get this straight, you haven't had sex in three weeks and expect me to believe that?" she asked, her tone a playful challenge.

He sighed heavily, the sound mingling with a reluctant chuckle. "Yes! For the tenth time," he insisted, meeting her deep brown eyes, which were narrowed in mock suspicion.

"I'm not stupid, Chris. There was a reason for that, I want to hear it," Kira pressed, her lips curving into a smirk that signaled she wouldn't let this go easily.

"Damn," Chris cursed under his breath, scratching his head. He hated how easily she could read him. "I really don't want to tell you. It's embarrassing."

Kira's smile broadened, the warmth of her victory radiating from her radiant brown skin. "Now I really want to hear it," she declared triumphantly.

With a heavy sigh of defeat, Chris glanced away before confessing. "At a party, I tried to hook up with someone, but…" He trailed off, his cheeks warming with a flush.

"But…?" Kira nudged, leaning closer with interest clear in her voice.

"I couldn't…get it up," he admitted, his voice barely above a whisper. "Then later, I ended up masturbating to a pornstar who looked like you. I only get hard for you." The words tumbled out, and Chris braced himself for her reaction.

A slow, devilish smile spread across Kira's face, and she licked her lips, a glint of mischief in her eyes. She leaned over the center console, her hand reaching for him. "So, does this work, cause if it doesn't we're going to have a problem," she teased, her palm pressing against his growing erection.

Chris shuddered, a guttural sound escaping him as he felt his body responding to her touch. "Yup, that worked," he managed to grunt, nodding emphatically.

Their laughter filled the car, an easy, intimate sound. Kira continued her ministrations, biting her lower lip in concentration. Her hand moved with purpose, and Chris moaned, entranced by the sight of her.

Kira unbuckled his belt with skillful fingers. The zipper gave way next, and her hand slipped inside, wrapping around him. "God, I forgot how big you were," she whispered.

The cool air of the car contrasted with her warm touch, sending shivers down his spine.

"Kira," he groaned, appreciating the determined look in her eyes, the same focus she brought to everything she did, from tutoring to this moment of unexpected intimacy.

Chris closed his eyes, surrendering to the sensation of her hand on him, but a new wave of pleasure washed over him as he felt the warm wetness of her mouth enveloping his cock. His breath hitched, and he reached out instinctively, finding her curly locks, letting them slide between his fingers. This woman, who sparred with him with such passion, now took him to the edge of reason with her lips and tongue.

Chris's mind clouded as Kira's mouth worked with a voracity that matched her academic debates. "Fuck!" his expletives echoed in the confined space of the car, mingling with the sound of their heavy breathing. The intensity of his release took him by surprise, leaving him momentarily stripped of his usual swagger.

Kira's laughter, warm and genuine, filled the air as she glanced up at him, her hand returning to coax life back into his cock. It didn't take long; he was quickly pulsing under her touch, the familiar desire surging through his veins with renewed vigor.

"Damn, Kira..." Chris muttered, watching with hazy eyes as she shed her shorts and panties with an efficiency that spoke volumes about her determination. She straddled him, and the world reduced to the sensation of her lowering onto him. He groaned, deep and guttural, feeling every inch of himself enveloped by her warmth.

"Chris," she whispered his name for him like a secret shared between their locked gaze. Slowly, she began moving, each descent drawing a ragged breath from him. Chris's hands found her hips, guiding her rhythm as if they were performing their own silent dance.

He watched, mesmerized, as she peeled off her shirt, revealing the curves he'd fantasized about during those empty weeks. His fingers lingered over her skin, tracing the paths he'd missed, until he couldn't resist the pull of her breasts any longer. "I missed these tits," he confessed, his voice thick with longing. Each suckle, each flick of his tongue, was a testament to his hunger for her.

Kira's response was a crescendo of motion—her pace quickening, her cries punctuating the night. Chris felt the build-up, the inevitable crash that was coming, and he clung to it, to her, like a lifeline.

"Kira… I'm—" The words tangled on his lips as pleasure wracked his body. Her affirmation came in gasps, and together they tumbled over the edge, lost in the depths of each other.

As reality seeped back in, the steamy haze on the windows and the scent of sex were just background details to the fact that he was here, with her, in a way he hadn't been with anyone else. They kissed, a seal over the words he never thought he'd say, but now couldn't hold back.

"Be mine," he whispered, the commitment-phobe within him silenced by the force of what pulsed between them.

Chapter 28

Kira barely made it three steps out of the classroom before she was ambushed. A swarm of students surrounded her, voices overlapping, all of them talking at once.

"Kira! When did this happen?"

"Why didn't you tell anyone?"

"So you and Chris Morin are official now?"

Kira blinked, completely caught off guard. "What—what are you talking about?"

A girl from her psychology class leaned in, grinning. "Chris has been telling everyone today that you're his new girlfriend."

Kira's entire brain short-circuited.

"He—what?"

Another guy smirked. "Yeah, pretty much half the campus knows by now."

Kira felt her stomach flip. Not because she wasn't happy, but because Chris hadn't even asked her yet. And now the whole school thought they were together. Before she could even process the information, the crowd began to disperse and when she turned, she saw why.

Molly Hayes.

The blonde approached with her usual poised, confident stride, looking Kira up and down like she was assessing competition.

"Well," Molly said, folding her arms, "congratulations. He's clearly *head* over heels for you."

Kira narrowed her eyes, waiting for the catch.

Molly's lips curled into a sharp smirk. "Just be careful. He's a notorious playboy, and we both know how his relationships end."

Kira tilted her head, unfazed. "Yeah? Well, I plan on lasting more than three weeks."

Molly's smirk vanished, replaced with a sharp glare as she stepped closer. "Excuse me?"

Before she could get in Kira's face, a familiar voice cut through the tension.

"Back off, Molly."

Chris.

Kira glanced over her shoulder just as Chris strode up beside her, casually slipping an arm around her waist. His green eyes were locked on Molly, his usual playfulness replaced with a hard edge.

Molly looked between them, her jaw tensing, before scoffing. "Whatever."

She turned on her heel and strutted away, clearly fuming.

As soon as she was gone, Chris turned to Kira with a smirk. "Hey."

Before she could say anything, he leaned down and kissed her, right there in the middle of campus. When he pulled away, Kira gave him an incredulous look. "So… I heard the news."

Chris chuckled, completely unapologetic. "It's not like you were gonna say no."

Kira let out an exasperated laugh, shaking her head. "You are ridiculous."

Chris grinned, tugging her closer. "And yet, you're still here."

She rolled her eyes but couldn't stop smiling.

As they walked toward his car together, hand in hand, she realized something.

Maybe Chris Morin was ridiculous.

But somehow, he was hers.

Chapter 29

Chris's apartment smelled of garlic and rosemary, the remains of a meticulously prepared dinner lingering in the air. He cleared away the last of the plates, his movements unusually fidgety. Kira watched him from across the table, her deep brown eyes tracing the lines of tension in his shoulders.

"Kira," Chris began, his voice uncharacteristically tentative as he reached across the table to capture her hand. The warmth of his palm was reassuring yet charged with an unfamiliar nervous energy. He exhaled slowly, as if steadying himself. "I've never done this before...asked someone to be my girlfriend, I mean. It's always been...casual."

She raised an eyebrow, her usual no-nonsense demeanor tempered by a softness reserved for moments like these. His vulnerability was disarming, and she felt as though she were seeing him truly unmasked for the first time.

"Kira, you're different. With you, I don't want casual. I want...I want you."

The silence that followed was thick with anticipation. Kira couldn't help but tease the edge off the moment. "You're being incredibly awkward, you know?"

A sheepish grin crossed his lips, but his eyes held hers with unwavering sincerity. "So, will you be my girlfriend?"

"Yes," she replied, the word feeling surprisingly right on her tongue.

In a fluid motion, Chris stood and rounded the table. The space between them closed as he leaned down to capture her lips with his. Their kiss was an intricate dance, a playful nip, a tender brush, a forceful press. Each movement igniting a spark that threatened to set them ablaze.

With a strength that belied his earlier nerves, Chris lifted Kira effortlessly, carrying her towards the bedroom. Her squeal of surprise transformed into laughter as she bounced on the mattress, the sound mingling with his low chuckle.

He hovered above her, tracing kisses along the exposed skin of her thighs, hidden only by the hem of her short black dress. The fabric bunched under his exploring hands, his mouth finding the heat of her through the thin barrier of her panties. Kira's moans filled the room with every lick of his tongue.

"Please," she panted, her words almost lost in the haze of pleasure. "I need more."

Chris groaned in response, pulling the obstructing fabric aside with a deliberate slowness that bordered on torture. Then, with a skill that had her gasping, he lavished attention upon her, his tongue painting strokes of ecstasy directly onto her trembling flesh.

"Chris…" Her fingers curled into the material of her dress, hiking it up, desperate to offer him every inch of herself. She teetered on the brink, the world narrowing to the point of his tongue against her clit.

But just before she could tumble over the edge, he paused, sitting back on his heels with a mischievous glint in his eye. Kira lay there, chest heaving, caught in the storm he'd conjured and craving its return.

Chris stood, his muscles flexing as he peeled his shirt over his head, revealing the tanned canvas of his broad chest. The sound of his belt clinking was like a starting bell, setting Kira's heart racing even faster. His jeans followed, the fabric whispering its descent to the floor, leaving him exposed and ready.

Kira watched, her breath caught in her throat, as Chris's hand wrapped around himself—hard, heavy, undeniable. He glanced at the foil square resting on the nightstand, then back at her.

"Forget it," she murmured, voice thick with desire. "I need you now."

A growl rumbled from Chris's chest, primal and approving. The corner of his mouth lifted in that cocky grin, the condom forgotten. Kneeling between her splayed legs, he aligned himself with her entrance, the tip teasing her before pressing forward.

"Look at me, Kira," he commanded gently as her eyelids fluttered, threatening to close. She fought against the wave of bliss, locking onto his piercing green eyes. Inch by deliberate inch, he slid into her, each movement deepening the connection that pulsed between them.

Her back arched off the bed, and she gripped his shoulders, nails digging crescents into his skin. "Chris…" The word was a plea.

"Shhh," he whispered, his voice a soothing balm as he started to move. "I know." His thrusts were deep and slow, a testament to the hunger they both felt. It was adoration painted in the strokes of physical desire.

"Deeper," Kira gasped, throwing her head back as her body welcomed him fully. Her thighs glistened with arousal, evidence of the storm he stirred within her. Every muscle in Chris's body coiled with the effort to remain controlled, to savor every second of their union.

"Only for you," he breathed into her ear, picking up the rhythm. Each thrust became a promise, a silent vow that this was more than physical—that what they shared go beyond the casual encounters that once defined him.

And with every push and pull, every whispered word and shared glance, they fell deeper into a passion that neither could deny.

Kira's breath hitched as she felt her bodys approaching climax, Chris's thrusts growing fiercer, each one an electric jolt that shot through her. She moaned, a sound mixed with insatiable desire and unspoken pleas for more. With reckless abandon, her legs found their way around his waist, drawing him impossibly closer, urging him to claim every inch of her.

"Chris!" Her voice broke the silence, a loud exclamation that rippled into the night. He answered her call with a deep chuckle, his lips seizing hers in a passionate kiss that swallowed her cries. Their tongues danced in a heated tangle, a wild rhythm that matched his relentless pace.

"Ri-right there," Kira gasped between kisses, her nails raking down his back as he repeatedly struck that perfect spot within her. "This your spot?" he managed between labored breaths, accentuating each word with a punishing thrust that sent waves of pleasure coursing through her.

"Yes!" she cried out, her body tightening around him like a vise, signaling the approach of her climax. "Fuck yeah," Chris growled, his own release nearing as he redoubled his efforts, the bed frame creaking in protest beneath them. Together they spiraled, a simultaneous release that left them shuddering, clutching at each other as if to anchor themselves amidst the storm of sensations.

As the aftershocks subsided, Chris reluctantly withdrew, only for his eyes to feast on the sight before him – his come spilling from her pussy and onto the sheets. "Shit...That's hot," he muttered, arousal reigniting within him at the raw display of their union.

Without missing a beat, Chris's hands were on her again, lifting her leg over his shoulder as he positioned himself at her entrance. With a groan punctuating the air, he slid back inside her, each stroke deep and merciless. "Seeing my come spill out of you, so fucking hot, baby," he breathed, his voice thick with lust.

Kira could only manage a throaty moan in reply, lost in the sensation of him filling her once more. "Are you gonna come for me again?" His words were both question and command, sending a thrill through her as she met his fevered gaze.

"Fuck yeesss," she confirmed, her body responding to his erratic movements, her heart racing in tandem with their joined flesh. They moved together, a passionate dance that ended in another shared climax, their cries mingling in the charged air as his seed spilled forth once more, marking them both.

Spent, they collapsed together, limbs entwined, hearts still pounding. "We need to get you on the pill asap so we can do this again," Chris said, his voice husky with satiation.

She chuckled, the sound rich with contentment. "I'm already on it." The revelation made Chris turn to her, pulling her close with renewed vigor. A wicked grin spread across his face.

"Then what are we waiting for?" His cock stiffened with anticipation, ready to worship her body all over again, as the night promised to be a long one.

Chapter 30

The sun hung low in the sky, painting the horizon in shades of orange, pink, and gold as Chris's car cruised down the open road. The windows were rolled down, letting in the warm evening breeze, and the hum of the engine mixed with the soft beat of music playing from the speakers.

Kira sat in the passenger seat, her legs tucked up on the seat, her face turned toward the window as she watched the sun dip lower.

It was peaceful. Something she hadn't expected when she started this whole thing with Chris Morin.

"Alright," Chris said, breaking the comfortable silence. "Tell me the truth. How annoying are my teammates?"

Kira snorted. "On a scale from one to complete chaos?"

Chris grinned. "Obviously complete chaos."

She sighed dramatically. "Then a solid twelve."

Chris laughed, drumming his fingers on the steering wheel. "Yeah, well, they're not wrong, you know."

Kira raised a brow. "About?"

He shot her a quick glance, his green eyes flickering with something soft. "You and me."

She hesitated, her fingers brushing against the hem of her dress. "What do you mean?"

Chris sighed, one hand still on the wheel as he reached over and laced their fingers together. "I mean, I get why you didn't think I was serious at first. Hell, I didn't even think I was capable of this before you."

Kira stayed quiet, her heart fluttering.

"But," he continued, squeezing her hand, "turns out? I really like having you around, Kira."

Kira smirked, squeezing his hand back. "Good. Because you're kinda stuck with me now."

Chris chuckled. "That supposed to be a threat?"

"More like a warning."

He grinned. "Noted."

They drove in comfortable silence, the kind that didn't need words, where everything was already understood. They'd deal with the drama—Molly's bitterness, Chris' teammates' relentless teasing, their own stubbornness. Right now, being together was the only thing they cared about.

As the sun finally dipped below the horizon, Chris lifted their joined hands and pressed a slow, lingering kiss to Kira's knuckles. "Whatever comes next," he murmured, "we'll figure it out."

Kira smiled, leaning her head back against the seat.

They would.

Together.

Also by Royal Reeds

Ride A Cowboy: A Short Erotic Story

When city girl Dali Neal breaks down on a rural highway, the last thing she expects is to be rescued by Hunter Bell, a ruggedly handsome Southern cowboy with a heart of gold. What starts as a simple act of kindness turns into something neither of them can ignore.

A short, steamy, small-town romance full of sizzling chemistry, and a cowboy who knows how to handle his woman just right.

Roommates: A Short Erotic Story

Millie has a problem…she's trying to write the ultimate spicy romance novel, but there's just one issue… she's never actually been satisfied herself.

Enter Jasper and Benjamin, her two ridiculously gorgeous roommates, who are more than willing to help her find the inspiration she desperately needs. What starts as a simple favor quickly turns into a night of passion that none of them can forget.

Lines blur, desires ignite, and Millie soon realizes that the best stories aren't just written, they're lived.

A short, very spicy romance that turns up the heat and refuses to turn it down.

105

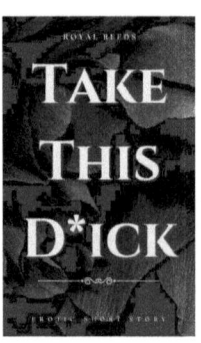

Take This D*ck: A Short Erotic Story

A sizzling romance unfolds between Alisha Price, a stunning bookstore owner, and Soren Sharpe, a fiery CEO who isn't used to hearing the word "no."

Get ready for a steamy tale of passion, power, and seduction that will leave your heart racing—and your e-reader practically smoking.